A DEADLY GAME

Janet Lorimer

PAGETURNERS

SUSPENSE

Boneyard
The Cold, Cold Shoulder
The Girl Who Had Everything
Hamlet's Trap
Roses Red as Blood

DETECTIVE

The Case of the Bad Seed
The Case of the Cursed Chalet
The Case of the Dead Duck
The Case of the Wanted Man
The Case of the Watery Grave

ADVENTURE

A Horse Called Courage
Planet Doom
The Terrible Orchid Sky
Up Rattler Mountain
Who Has Seen the Beast?

SCIENCE FICTION

Bugged!
Escape from Earth
Flashback
Murray's Nightmare
Under Siege

MYSTERY

The Hunter
Once Upon a Crime
Whatever Happened to Megan Marie?
When Sleeping Dogs Awaken
Where's Dudley?

SPY

A Deadly Game
An Eye for an Eye
I Spy, e-Spy
Scavenger Hunt
Tuesday Raven

Development and Production: Laurel Associates, Inc.

ISBN-13: 978-1-56254-136-1
ISBN-10: 1-56254-136-6
eBook: 978-1-60291-239-7

Printed in the United States of America
16 15 14 13 12 11 2 3 4 5 6 7

CONTENTS

Chapter 1

Jim Salvatori sensed trouble as he climbed out of his car. He'd parked in one of the campus parking slots marked *Computer Security*. Now he wished he'd parked on the street. He'd been warned that not everyone at Mayfair College would welcome him.

As he locked his car, Jim looked around cautiously. He saw a handful of students watching him. He smiled at them, but not one of them smiled back. A couple of the guys muttered to each other as they glared at Jim. He decided it was best to ignore them—as long as they left his car alone.

Jim pulled a map of the campus from his pocket. When he'd interviewed for this job, he'd taken a quick tour. It was a huge campus that sprawled over dozens of acres. Now, a week later, Jim was having a hard time remembering where everything was.

Jim admired the campus as he crossed it. Mayfair College was famous for its beautiful grounds. Wide paths cut through broad green lawns. Gardeners tended beds of colorful flowers. In the center of the campus, water leaped from a tall marble fountain into a clear pool.

Jim glanced at the buildings he passed. Most of them were made from brick, and many were quite old. He spotted the building where he would be working. He was about to go inside when something hit the back of his head. The missile was soft. Jim wasn't hurt, but the blow startled him.

He turned quickly. A small group of students stood about 10 feet away. They watched in silence as Jim looked down. A banana peel lay on the ground. Jim picked up the limp, brownish peel and dropped it into a nearby trash can.

Two or three of the students laughed. Jim ignored them. He knew why they were upset. But going after him was not about to solve their problem. He pushed open the door and went inside.

Jim found himself in a fairly new building. It had been built to house the college's first, enormous mainframe computers. Now, less than 20 years later, computers of all sizes dominated the campus.

Like most other institutions in the world, Mayfair College had become totally dependent on computers. They were used to keep student records up-to-date. The Accounting Department used computers to keep track of income and expenses. Students used computers to do research and finish assignments. And, of course, the campus hospital used computers to keep track of patients' records.

Just a few weeks before, computers all over campus had been attacked by a computer virus. When people tried to do their work, a cartoon of a ladybug appeared on screen. The virus became known as the Love Bug. It quickly spread from one computer to the next, slowing down all the systems on campus until the virus was finally erased.

The president of Mayfair—Dr. Allan Delaney—decided to step up computer security. This started an ongoing battle between people who wanted the security and those who did not.

Most of the students and a few of the professors were dead set against more rules and regulations. They believed it was important to keep the system as open as possible. It was easier to share information this way. Jim figured that people from this group were behind the banana peel missile.

Other people believed that computer users should have privacy. They claimed that leaving the system wide open was an invitation to spies, thieves, and all other kinds of mischief-makers.

It was an old argument—one that had never been resolved. But this time, President Delaney had insisted on having his way. He made a decision to create the brand new Computer Security Department. He had interviewed a lot of good people to head up the department. In the end, he had hired Jim Salvatori. Why? Jim Salvatori had a dark secret—something that made him the perfect choice for the job.

Chapter 2

Jim paused in the doorway of the Computer Security Department. The day he had first toured the campus, he had taken only a quick look around the big basement room. Now he let his gaze travel slowly around the room.

Greenish-white fluorescent bulbs provided the only light. There were no windows. One end of the room had been divided into workstations. Each cubicle contained a desk with a computer terminal and a chair. The other end of the room housed the giant mainframes. The place was functional, not attractive.

Jim closed the door behind him. Three people—two young men and a young woman—were grouped around one terminal. As Jim walked into the middle of the room, they turned to stare at him. Then one of the men stepped forward, hand outstretched.

"Mr. Salvatori? Welcome aboard. I'm Pete Harris," the greeter said with a smile. As they shook hands, Jim sized Pete up. The guy looked like he was in his middle twenties. His hair was tied back in a neat ponytail and he was wearing a clean shirt and slacks. He looked intelligent and alert. Jim sensed that Pete was serious about his work.

"Hey there, Cybercop," the girl said sarcastically. "I'm Tori O'Neal, at your command."

"Tori!" Pete exclaimed, looking a little embarrassed.

"That's okay," Jim said with a grin. Tori looked about 20 years old. It was hard to tell what color her hair really was because it had been dyed so many colors. She wore a nose ring, heavy eye makeup, thigh-high boots, and a smart-alecky sneer. Everything about her screamed, "Rebel without a clue!"

Steve Klein was the third worker. Steve appeared to be in his late teens. He was the stereotype of a computer nerd—a bright kid with glasses, a bad haircut, and a pocket protector. He wore jeans and a rumpled white shirt.

"We've been trying to hold down the fort until you arrived, Mr. Salvatori," Pete said, "but we weren't sure . . . " His voice trailed away.

Jim realized they were waiting for him to take over. He smiled. "First, call me Jim. When people use my last name, I always look around to see if my father's in the room."

Steve and Pete laughed nervously at Jim's lame stab at humor. Tori rolled her eyes and look bored.

"Okay," Jim said, "would one of you show me my workstation? Then maybe you can tell me about the security system you've got here."

His words struck the right note. Even

Tori seemed to thaw out a few degrees.

Jim picked a cubicle no one else was using and dropped off his briefcase. After that, Pete gave Jim a quick tour of the room. Jim could tell that Computer Security had been hastily put together.

"Right now we're just trying to manage the system," Pete said. "We help new users set up secure accounts. We try to make sure the system keeps running smoothly." He shrugged. "And of course if someone *does* hack in, we do our best to repair the damage. But that hasn't happened lately."

"The trouble is—until we catch the hacker, we're always one step behind," Jim said. "We need to get *ahead* of him somehow. Plug the holes in advance, you know?"

Steve and Tori had gone back to their workstations. As Jim passed their cubicles, he glanced at their monitors. It looked like Steve was checking accounts. But Tori seemed to be writing a program.

Jim wondered what her program was for, but he was reluctant to ask. Jim sighed. He'd never been anyone's boss before. These students weren't much younger than he was. How was he supposed to talk to them?

At that moment, a phone rang. "I'll get it," Tori said. She unfolded her long, lean frame and strolled across the room to a wall phone.

Jim winced when she answered the phone with, "Joe's Grill and Computer Security." It looked like they needed to have a meeting to set up a few rules. He knew only too well how college students like to operate.

Then Tori put her hand over the mouthpiece. "Hey, Cybercop!" she said to Jim. "It's for you. It's the Bulldog!" For the first time, she grinned.

Chapter 3

Cybercop? Jim raised one eyebrow as he took the receiver. If Tori knew he was annoyed, she didn't show it.

The "Bulldog" turned out to be Mrs. Barlow in the Administration Department. She was calling to make a complaint. Someone had hacked into the college's administration records the night before. "At least I have to *assume* that's when it happened," she snapped. "All I know for certain is that someone has been making changes in the records."

It was one of Mrs. Barlow's jobs to send out notices to any students who weren't making the grade. She explained that several students taking a philosophy course were failing.

"Yesterday I planned to send those

students warning notices," Mrs. Barlow said. "If they don't bring up their grades, they'll be dropped from the class. It's a routine notice that we send out in the middle of the semester. We do that for all the departments. But when I went into the records this morning, I found that every student taking philosophy was passing."

"Did you keep a list of which students were failing?" Jim asked.

"No—not separate from the computer records," Mrs. Barlow replied.

"Well, what about the teacher?" Jim asked. "Doesn't he have a list of the students who are failing? He must have kept one."

"On the computer," Mrs. Barlow said.

"Well, I see your problem," Jim said. "You aren't going to like the next question—but I have to ask. Did you back up these records on disks?"

Mrs. Barlow groaned. "No, I'm afraid I didn't. I don't know if Dr. Scott did.

He's the head of the department."

"Okay, Mrs. Barlow," Jim said. "We'll try to check it out from our end."

As he hung up, he saw Pete, Tori, and Steve watching him. He told them what had just happened.

Pete and Steve glanced at each other and nodded. "Sounds like Harry's back at work," Steve said.

Jim frowned. "Harry?"

Steve grinned. "Harry the Hacker. That's what we call the guy who hacked in a while back. The one we're trying to catch. But, of course, *he* could be a *she*," Steve went on, giving Tori a teasingly suspicious look.

She stuck out her tongue.

"Pete, I need to see the records of all the users," Jim said. "But first, let's go over the system together. I need to understand *exactly* how Mayfair has designed its computer-user system."

Pete seemed more than happy to help. It turned out that Jim was already familiar with the kind of system Mayfair used. Each user was signed up with an account number. And each user, of course, picked a password.

"Those safeguards are supposed to make it hard for hackers to get into the system," Pete said.

Jim laughed and shook his head. "But of course it doesn't. A clever hacker can sneak right in."

"Every time a user spends time on the computer," Pete went on, "a record is made of the time used. Then, at the end of the month, each user gets a bill. You know, just like an electric bill."

Jim nodded. "Does every department follow the same plan?"

Steve chuckled. "You *wish!* The fact is that lots of departments are sloppy about their record keeping."

Tori agreed. "And as for passwords," she said, "they're about as helpful as a trapdoor in a canoe."

Jim laughed. As annoying as Tori

could be, she did have a sense of humor.

"We tell everyone to change their passwords on a regular basis," Tori went on. "Do they? No! We tell them to keep their passwords secret, even from their friends. Do they? No! And we tell them their passwords should be a series of numbers, letters, or even symbols. Do they pick difficult passwords? No!"

"So this really is a campus-wide problem?" Jim asked. Steve and Pete nodded. "Well, it's time we changed all that," Jim said firmly.

"D'ya mind if I ask a question?" Tori looked as if she expected an argument.

"Go for it," Jim said warily.

"We've been trying to figure out why President Delaney hired you," Tori said. "What makes you—an outsider—better suited than one of us to head up this department?"

Chapter 4

Jim gazed at Tori with a blank expression. Then he said, "That will have to wait, Tori. We don't have time to discuss it right now. Maybe later."

The others exchanged quick glances. Jim knew that the less he opened up, the harder it would be for him. But, unfortunately, that was part of his arrangement with Delaney. Until the hacker was caught, Jim Salvatori's past would have to remain a mystery.

Pete was the first to accept Jim's answer. "Well, then—that's it. Let's get to work," he said.

Pete and Jim went off to check out the computer-user records of the Administration Department. Tori and Steve followed along.

"I don't see a single password I don't recognize," Pete said in dismay. Then he explained in more detail. "I worked here in Admin last summer. The secretaries almost *never* changed their passwords. Take a look at this. I can tell you right now that all the users who logged on yesterday are people I know."

"But those are daytime users," Jim said. "I don't think our hacker would have gone into student records during working hours, do you? Let's look for a late-night entry."

Pete found that someone had logged on after midnight. "I doubt that one would have been a secretary," he chuckled. "I know the secretaries are loyal and hard-working and all that. But they don't get paid enough to hang around working after midnight!"

Jim laughed.

"But it *is* an authentic password for one of the workers," Pete went on. "I know that password, in fact. I've told the user half a dozen times that she needs to change it."

Tori leaned over his shoulder to look at the monitor. "After you do this for a while," she told Jim, "you get to know a lot of the users. And it doesn't take much guesswork to figure out their passwords. In fact, we often make a little game of it."

Steve scooted his chair back from his terminal so he could join in on the conversation. "Tell me the name of your dog, your kid, and when you were born. I'll tell you your password before you can say 'top secret'."

Jim shook his head and smiled. He knew that Steve was right. People just didn't stop to think when they picked a password. "You don't happen to keep a list of the administration passwords, do you?" he asked.

"No, the users are responsible for their own passwords," Tori said. "We leave it up to each user to choose a password and then remember it. They *are* supposed to change their passwords on a regular basis. But even if they did, we'd never have the time to keep a list like that up to date."

"Okay," Jim said, pushing back his chair. He stood up and stretched. "It looks like Mayfair is relying on an old-fashioned system for keeping computer records safe. What about Biometrics?"

Pete whistled in disbelief. Steve whooped and Tori's jaw dropped. "Biometrics? Wow!" she yelled.

"It's a much better system," Jim said. "I bet you've seen it used in some of the high-tech movies. You know, like James Bond films—where fingerprints or voiceprints are used to identify a user."

"Oh, we *know* what the Biometrics system is," Tori said sharply. "But do you know what that would cost?"

Jim nodded. "Sure, it's expensive. But you get what you pay for."

Pete laughed. "You don't really know

old Scrooge Delaney very well, do you? He couldn't bear to part with so many of the school's precious dollars."

Jim's eyebrow shot up. "Even if it means protecting important records?"

"Oh, get real!" Tori straddled the chair in her cubicle. "Delaney would much rather hire us. He pays us almost nothing. Then he screams at us when the hacker gets into the records."

"Yeah. We're the computer security scapegoats," Steve said. "Are you sure you still want this job, Jim?"

Jim grinned. "You bet," he said. "I love a good challenge." He got to his feet. "Look, I'd better go talk to the—" He turned and shot a hard look at Tori. "—the Bulldog?"

Tori grinned and nodded. "Once you meet Barlow, you'll understand. And in her case, the dog's bite really *is* worse than her bark. But you're a full-fledged adult, and we're just students. She *may* be a lot nicer to you."

When Jim got to the Administration building, he found Mrs. Barlow with Dr. Scott, the philosophy professor. He wasn't being very "philosophical" about the altered grades.

"How can I run my department if someone is going to tamper with the records?" he roared.

Mrs. Barlow growled and snapped. "Don't complain to *me,* Dr. Scott! You should direct your complaints to—" Then she spotted Jim, and the Bulldog attacked. Jim let the two of them snarl at him for a couple of minutes. Then he asked them why they'd failed to back up their records. Mrs. Barlow and Dr. Scott quickly backed off.

"I'm working on a computer program to find and plug security holes in our system," Jim said. "That will help—but it won't solve all the problems. Each of you will have to do your share, too."

Dr. Scott drew back, as if Jim had threatened him. "I'm a teacher, not a cop!" he growled. "That's *your* job."

"We have to work together," Jim said patiently. "All I'm saying is that you people have to be on guard, too. You need to pay close attention to who uses the terminals in your department. Is anyone logging on who shouldn't be? Is there a good reason why one account is used a lot more often than it should be? It would be a big help if you'd keep track of what your students are doing."

Dr. Scott glared at Jim. "I believe in freedom of information," he said in a huffy tone. "In fact, I believe the hacker has a *right* to hack into the system!"

Chapter 5

Jim stared at Dr. Scott as if he couldn't believe his ears. "You're in favor of students breaking into—"

When Dr. Scott saw the look on Jim's face, he hurried on. "Oh, I don't mean the hacker has the right to change the records. But most hackers live by a code of ethics. They do no damage. They're just bright kids who want to see if they have the skills to crack the system."

Jim raised an eyebrow. He'd heard this argument before. "I understand your point. Hackers versus crackers," he said. "Hackers break in just for the fun of it. Crackers are the computer criminals."

"So the person who changed those files was a cracker, not a hacker!" Mrs. Barlow exclaimed.

Jim shrugged. "Even hackers can do a lot of damage. They may not *mean* to—but they've been known to erase files accidentally."

"So go catch the cracker," Dr. Scott snapped. "Or hacker. But please don't try to make me do your work for you." He stormed out of the office.

Jim turned to Mrs. Barlow. "I need a list of all the students taking philosophy this semester," he said. "Could you help me with that?"

Mrs. Barlow's face brightened. "That won't be hard to do," she said. "Do you have a few minutes?"

While Mrs. Barlow printed out class rosters, Jim asked her to check for other changed grades. "You said that you send out warning notices to every student who's failing," he said.

Mrs. Barlow nodded. "That's right. Dr. Scott just happened to send us his list first," she said.

"You'll need to send a memo out to

all the departments," Jim said. "Remind them they need to back up their files."

Just as Jim was heading out the door, he saw President Delaney coming up the front steps. Delaney stopped Jim to ask for an update. "I hear the hacker is back at work," he said with a frown.

Jim nodded. Then he explained what he was doing to solve the problem. "I still think the hacker is a student," Jim said quietly. "Probably some kid who just wants to have some fun. And power! The hacker messed things up for the Philosophy Department when he changed the failing grades. Dr. Scott is pretty mad right now."

Delaney winced. "Now look here, Salvatori, you told me—"

"I told you I'd do my best," Jim snapped. "But don't forget—this is my first day on the job."

"What about those kids working in your department?" Delaney said. "What are they doing? You know that it's your job to make them toe the line."

"They're doing fine," Jim said. "But *you* may have to think about other types of computer security."

Delaney waved the suggestion away. "Nothing that costs money," he snapped.

Jim felt frustrated. He wanted to ask Delaney what his annual salary was, but he thought better of it.

"I'd better get back to work now," Jim said. Another minute of Delaney's unreasonable attitude and Jim was afraid he'd lose his temper.

"I assume you're settled in now. Is everything satisfactory?" Delaney asked.

Jim thought about the banana peel and the angry looks on some of the students' faces. "I can't say I was crazy about the welcoming committee," Jim said. "This doesn't seem to be the friendliest place to work."

Delaney's eyes narrowed. "Maybe not—but you don't have much choice, now do you?" he sneered.

Jim was steamed. But letting Delaney get to him wouldn't find the hacker. He sat on a bench and pulled out the class lists Mrs. Barlow had given him. He went over the names of the students. There weren't many philosophy classes being offered this semester, and all the classes were small.

Then, a familiar name caught Jim's eye—*Victoria O'Neal.* "Well, well," Jim thought. "If it isn't our Tori." He hadn't thought of her as a philosophy student. He'd figured a girl like her would be studying either art or drama.

Seeing Tori's name on the class roster made Jim stop and think. *She* might be the hacker! She'd have a motive to change the students' grades—especially if she was failing the course herself.

"But if that's the case," Jim thought, "I'd better check on Steve and Pete, too."

Jim knew that the hacker could be anyone—on campus or off. But he had to start somewhere.

When he got back to the security center, Jim found a student reporter waiting for him.

"We cover all the news that's *fair* to print," the reporter said. "May*fair* to print, that is." Then he chuckled at his own awful joke. Tori rolled her eyes, and Steve made a gagging sound.

Jim tried to cooperate. He wanted to make life easier for himself and his co-workers. If the students felt he was on their side, it could be a big help. And Jim knew that, at the moment, they considered him the enemy.

The reporter got right to the point. "How do you feel about the students' right to freely share information through the computer?" he asked.

Jim smiled. "That's what we would like to see happen in an ideal situation," he said. "The trouble is that computers are used for so many different purposes. And some of those purposes require privacy. For example, a hacker could break into a bank's computers to read your bank balance."

The reporter laughed loudly. "Hey, that's no secret," he said. "I've got 54 dollars and—"

Steve and Tori broke out in whoops of laughter. Jim waited until they calmed down. "Not everyone feels the same way," he said patiently. "If you aren't interested in keeping your finances quiet, what secrets do you have?"

The reporter stared at Jim coldly. "I don't have any secrets," he said.

Jim was glad when Pete stepped in. "What's your senior project?" Pete asked the reporter.

The student turned his blank stare on Pete. "Why?"

"What if you had put in months of research?" Pete said. "Suppose you finally got the report written, and you turned it in. But the teacher flunked you because someone else turned in the same report. The teacher figured *you* used your computer to steal that information from the other student."

The reporter's face turned red. "Man, that's *ugly!*"

Pete nodded. "Well, it *could* happen, buddy. That's what Jim means by a right to privacy. Sure, it's good to share information. No one doubts that! But some people carry it too far. They just *take* whatever they want. And that's stealing—no matter how you look at it."

As the reporter started to scribble in his notebook, Jim began to think that the worst was over. Then the student asked the question Jim had been dreading. "Okay, Mr. Salvatori, I need to get some information about you and your background."

Chapter 7

Jim tried to stall. "There's not much to tell," he stammered. "I was born, I went to school, I—"

He knew that Pete, Steve, and Tori were watching him closely.

Then suddenly the phone rang. Tori went to answer it.

"Saved by the bell," Jim thought. He could feel beads of sweat forming on his forehead. He smiled lamely at the reporter as he waited to find out who was calling.

"Hey, Jim!" Tori called out. "Harry the Hacker seems to have struck again. This time it's the hospital!"

Mayfair College Hospital was famous for its new techniques and cutting-edge therapies. It was a teaching hospital that took in very ill patients. If the hacker messed up their records, it could mean death for innocent people.

Jim sprang out of his chair and crossed the room. He grabbed the phone, introduced himself, and listened.

The news was grim. The hacker had apparently planted a virus. Fortunately, the virus had only slowed things down so far. But nurses and doctors were having trouble getting into the patients' medical records. The hospital director sounded angry and frustrated.

"I'd better get right over there and take a look," Jim said.

As Jim hurried across campus, he thought about how his day was going. Already he'd run into two sets of problems with the hacker. "The first break-in was just a few weeks ago," Jim thought to himself. "Now, just today, there are two more. Harry seems to be stepping up his program."

But *why?* That was what it always

boiled down to. Was Harry the Hacker nothing more than a bored student? Or was he much more dangerous than that? Was Harry trying to get even with the school for something? Maybe Harry was a student who had flunked out.

So far Harry hadn't gained much from the attacks. Jim thought again about the students who were failing the philosophy class. But that couldn't have been the only thing on the hacker's mind, or he would have stopped there. Why bother with an annoying virus in the hospital computers? What did that have to do with changing grades in a different department? Unless . . .

Just outside the hospital, Jim came to a sudden stop. Was it possible there were *two* hackers? Or maybe a group? That was something else to consider.

Inside the busy hospital, Jim found the director waiting for him. Ms. Clay was clearly angry. "So far this virus doesn't seem to have done much damage," she said, "but it *could*. Mr. Salvatori, when are you going to catch the hacker?"

"I'm working on it right now," Jim assured her. "And when I do," he thought, "I'm going to—" He wouldn't let himself finish the thought.

When they got to Ms. Clay's office, she pointed silently at her monitor. A cartoon character dressed like a patient was dancing on the screen.

"Look! That's all it does," Ms. Clay said. "And when we try to get past it, everything slows down."

Jim sat down at the terminal and went to work. He knew that there were several ways for a computer to get a virus. One way was to download an infected file from the Internet. Another way was to use an infected floppy disk.

Jim began to question Ms. Clay about the hospital's computer system. As she talked, Jim realized that the hacker would have had to come into the hospital to plant the "infection."

"We aren't hooked into the campus system," Ms. Clay explained. "We have our own in-house system, you see."

"That's interesting," Jim said, "and useful to know. It's possible that our hacker left 'footprints' when he infected your system."

Ms. Clay frowned. *"Footprints?* I don't understand. Not real ones, surely?"

Jim smiled. "No, I'm talking about telltale tracks the hacker left behind when he created the virus and—"

At that moment, the door flew open. A nurse burst into the room. Her face was as white as her scrubs. "Ms. Clay, you need to come with me at once. We have a—" She glanced at Jim.

"It's all right," Ms. Clay said impatiently. "What's happened?"

"It's Professor Anderson. He was given the wrong dose of medication by accident and—" She paused. "We've got a medical team working on him, but—" She shook her head.

Chapter 8

Ms. Clay groaned. "What next? Okay, I'm coming." She turned to Jim. "I'm sorry, Mr. Salvatori, but I'll have to leave you on your own for a while."

After Ms. Clay left, Jim went to work at the computer. The deeper he dug into the infected program, the more interesting it got. He examined the whole thing carefully, looking for something that might tell him more about the hacker. For one thing, he noticed that the program had been loaded at night. If this were the same hacker, he was pretty busy after dark.

By studying the program a little longer, Jim picked up some clues about the way it was written. He learned that the same person who had changed the philosophy grades had also written this program. That suggested that one person was doing all the mischief on campus!

On the other hand, making it hard to take care of sick people was no prank. Why had the hacker planted a virus in the hospital system? Didn't he realize he was playing with people's lives?

"This character thinks he's pretty smart," Jim thought. "But at least I've figured out a way to lock him out of the hospital system."

Jim went to find Ms. Clay, to let her know what he planned to do.

He spotted a nurse in the hallway and asked if she could help him get a message to Ms. Clay. He explained why.

The nurse smiled. "If there's anything I can do to help, just let me know," she said. "In fact, if you want someone to hang the hacker by his toes—I'll be thrilled to do that, too!" The anger in her tone was obvious.

Jim raised an eyebrow, and she

spelled it out. "One of our patients—Professor Anderson—almost died a while ago. He came *this close.*" She held her thumb and first finger close together. "It was an accident that never should have happened."

"How *did* it happen?" Jim asked.

"Someone messed around with his chart. We're guessing that it was your hacker up to his usual mischief."

Jim winced. "Hey, he's not *my* hacker," he cried. "Tell me what he did."

"He changed the amount of medicine Professor Anderson was supposed to get!" she cried in an outraged voice.

"Slow down," Jim said. "You mean that kind of information is being kept on the computer?"

"Of course," the nurse replied. "The nurse who usually takes that shift was out sick. So the nurse who came in to give the professor his medicine didn't realize that the chart was wrong. Almost at once, Professor Anderson had a bad reaction. After the medical team got him stabilized, we checked the records. Sure enough! The dose *had* been changed. That's when we figured out what must have happened."

"But the professor is okay now, isn't he?" Jim asked nervously.

The nurse shook her head slowly. "He's not completely out of danger. And what a shame! Professor Anderson is a brilliant man. Why, just a few months ago he published an award-winning article in a science journal. He's really something special!"

Jim whistled. "Do you remember the subject of his article?"

The woman frowned. "Something to do with computers. Funny, isn't it? The professor is an *expert* on computers—and now it's another computer expert that almost does him in!"

The hacker's tricks were turning deadly. If Jim and his team didn't stop him soon, someone might die!

Jim left the hospital and hurried back to his own department. He spent the rest of the day writing a security program. Then he made a note to remind himself to also check the hospital's system for guest log-ins and other accounts that might be suspect. He barely noticed when Pete, Steve, and Tori said goodnight and left.

When he finally finished his work, Jim shoved his chair back. He gazed at the screen in satisfaction. "There! That should take care of you, Harry," he muttered.

Now all he had to do was install the new program in the hospital computers, and then he could go home. He glanced up at the wall clock and did a double take! He hadn't realized how much time had gone by. No wonder his stomach was growling.

Heading toward the hospital, Jim hurried across the darkening campus. Lights flickered on in all the buildings.

Small groups of students were crossing the campus, most of them heading for night classes.

As Jim walked up to the hospital, he thought about the hacker. "What kind of guy is he? What is he after? I need to come up with some kind of profile," he thought. "That might help me narrow the field of suspects. And I need to do some serious checking into the records."

But all of that was going to take time. The trouble was, Jim didn't know how much time he had left.

Chapter 9

After installing the security program on the hospital computer system, Jim felt exhausted. He decided that everything else could wait. He needed to go home, get a bite to eat, and relax.

As long as he was there, however, he wanted to check on Professor Anderson. He was relieved to learn that the professor was doing better.

While he was talking to the nurse on duty, Jim spotted Ms. Clay coming out of her office. He told her about installing the new security program, and she looked hopeful for the first time. "Does that mean we won't be having any more problems?" she asked.

Jim shrugged. "I sure hope not—but nothing is foolproof. By the way, I understand that one of your patients almost died because of the hacker."

Ms. Clay nodded grimly. "I've alerted campus security," she said, "but there's not much that anyone can do right now. As far as I know, there are no suspects."

"The virus software was loaded into the system from a terminal right here in the hospital," Jim said. "Who knows? The hacker may have used that same terminal to break into patient records. Also, the hacker may have been a visitor. Did anyone here notice anything—or anyone—unusual the other night?"

The director shook her head. "I've talked to everyone who was on duty. We don't remember any unauthorized person trying to use one of our computers. But we have dozens of terminals—even downstairs in the morgue! And we don't have anyone on duty in the morgue at night."

"Are visitors required to sign in?" Jim asked.

Ms. Clay seemed to brighten up. "As a matter of fact, they are. Let's go take a look at the sign-in book."

Ms. Clay led Jim down the hall to the nurses' station. A waiting area for visitors was off to the side. Jim was surprised to see Steve reclining in one of the chairs. He was reading a paperback with a sensational cover. "Hey, Steve," Jim said. "I thought you'd gone home."

Steve looked up, startled. When he saw Jim, bright spots of color rose in his cheeks.

"Don't tell me you're here to see one of the patients," Jim said.

Steve looked nervous. Turning an even deeper shade of red, he said, "Uh—just waiting for a friend to get off work."

"One of the nurses' aides," Ms. Clay whispered. "He waits for her, and then walks her to her dorm."

"See you tomorrow," Jim said to Steve. He followed Ms. Clay behind the counter of the nurses' station to look at the guest book. "How long has Steve been hanging around here in the evenings?" he asked softly.

"Oh, a couple of weeks, I guess," Ms. Clay replied. "Whenever the girl works a late shift. After a while he kind of became part of the furniture, you know? We just forget he's here."

"Hmmm. That could have been what the hacker did," Jim thought to himself. "Maybe he hung around until people got used to seeing him."

Jim glanced up and down the hall. It would take no time at all to slip into an empty office and load an infected disk into the computer. But the hacker had also hacked into the records.

"Here's the visitor sign-in book," said Ms. Clay. "You know, Jim, until a few months ago, we never required people to sign in when they came to visit. But now campus security makes us track visitors."

Jim nodded. He began to check names, going back to the day when the professor had been admitted. He knew that it was possible to make a virus that wouldn't show itself until someone accidentally triggered it.

He saw a few names he recognized, including Steve's. Then he saw that President Delaney had come to visit Professor Anderson. As much as Jim wanted the hacker to be Delaney, he knew that there wasn't a chance. Delaney just wasn't clever enough.

Jim moved down the page. Pete Harris had come to visit several nights before the virus had been installed. So had Professor Scott. Even Tori O'Neal had been in the hospital the night before the virus was triggered. "Back to square one," Jim thought.

After Jim left the hospital, he went home. He shared a small apartment overlooking the city with his cat, Fido. The view and playing with Fido were two of Jim's favorite things.

Jim fixed something to eat and took

his plate onto the balcony. Fido jumped onto the arm of his chair. Jim gave the cat a handful of kitty treats. Then he gazed out at the city lights that sparkled like stars all the way to the horizon.

As he ate, Jim thought about the hacker breaking into computers. "It would be the same if some kind of spy broke into this apartment house," Jim told Fido. "Suppose it went this way: In each apartment, the spy opens drawers and paws through people's clothes. He goes through their closets. He looks at their photographs and reads their letters. Nothing is private."

Fido purred, rubbing his head against Jim's shoulder.

"Let's say this spy is not really a bad guy," Jim said. "Like the hacker, the spy is just having fun. Making mischief. Playing tricks on people. He's like a little kid who does something just to prove he can do it. The baffling thing is, this spy is *so* good, no one knows how he's getting into the apartments."

Fido climbed into Jim's lap, purring loudly. Jim put his empty plate on the floor next to his chair.

"Are you with me so far, Fido? Let's say the spy is desperate to show people how clever he is," Jim went on. "In order to attract attention, he has to leave a calling card."

He scratched Fido gently between his ears and let his imagination run free.

"At the same time, our spy doesn't want to get caught," Jim continued. "So he does something about that the next time he breaks in. Suppose he leaves a note in the lobby, telling people that he's the guy. But he signs it with a phony name. Something like *Cybercreep!*"

Fido meowed in agreement.

"Okay, okay. I agree," Jim said. "It's a pretty stupid name. But give me a break, Fido—it's late and I'm tired." Jim was quiet for a long time, thinking hard. "Okay, Fido, you've got me. What is it about this case that I'm missing?"

Jim and Fido sat in silence. The moon rose, and the air grew colder. Fido put his nose under his tail and went to sleep.

"Well, you're no help," Jim said. "Okay, let's see what we've got. A hacker. Files that are messed up. An annoying virus. And—"

Then suddenly it came to him. The Mayfair College spy, Harry the Hacker, had failed to leave a calling card.

Chapter 10

The next day Jim got to work before anyone else. His fingers were flying over his keyboard when Tori walked in.

She seemed surprised that he had arrived so early. "Trying to make a good impression?" she asked. "Or are you just showing off to set a good example?"

Jim grinned at her over his shoulder. "Wrong on both counts. Just trying to catch a hacker."

Tori grunted as she dumped her backpack on her chair.

"So tell me," Jim said. "How's your philosophy class going?"

Her eyes widened. "How did you—" Tori's mouth tightened in anger. "So *that's* why you came in early. To hack into my records," she snapped.

Then Jim heard the door open. He saw Steve standing in the doorway, staring uncertainly at Jim and Tori. Obviously, he'd heard Tori's raised voice. The tension in the room had stopped him short.

Jim's smile vanished as he turned back to Tori. "A hacker changed the failing grades of some students in the Philosophy Department. That's why I'm interested."

"So what's your point? You think *I* did it?" Her eyes narrowed in anger.

"You tell me," he said quietly.

She glared at him. "No, *you* figure it out, Cybercop!" She angrily snatched up her backpack. "I quit!"

"No!" Steve exclaimed. "You can't quit, Tori!" Then he turned to Jim. "You've got it all wrong, Jim. Tori doesn't *need* to change her grades. Didn't you know that she's an honors student? Has been for two years."

Jim's jaw dropped. "Honors?"

"What?" Tori snapped. "You don't think that someone who looks like me could be an honors student?" She was still upset, still defensive.

"I apologize," Jim said, standing up. "At the same time, that still doesn't let you off the hook. Nor you, Steve. And if you think being accused of hacking is funny, let me tell you what your Harry character has done now."

Jim quickly outlined what had happened to Professor Anderson the day before. "The hacker is now playing games with people's lives. Do you understand? If the professor dies, the hacker will be guilty of manslaughter."

Steve and Tori glanced at each other, then back at Jim.

"Each of you visited the hospital after Professor Anderson was admitted," Jim went on. "Either one of you could be the hacker. You're both smart enough and have enough experience. I had to eliminate you guys and Pete before I started looking somewhere else."

"Eliminate me from what?" Pete stood in the doorway, frowning at them.

Jim explained what he was doing.

Then Steve burst out impatiently, "Take a look at the hacker's work, Jim. Does the hacker's style of programming match any of our stuff?"

"Yeah!" Tori exclaimed. She perched on a corner of her desk. "And another thing, Cybercop—"

"Hey!" Jim said angrily. "It's time you quit calling me that."

"Okay," Tori agreed sullenly. "Jim, there's something else you need to know. All three of us took computer classes from Professor Anderson. It's just possible that a lot of our programming techniques are similar. But that's going to be true for a lot of students."

Jim thought about it. "I guess that's right," he said. "What do you suggest?"

"There must be another common denominator somewhere," Pete said slowly. "You know—something that links everything the hacker has been doing to the same person."

"Well, let's get to work," Jim said. "Drop everything else. I want you guys to put all your energy into trying to narrow the field."

"What about the user accounts?" Tori said. "What about—"

"I'll take care of the drudge work," Pete said. Then, with a wry smile, he explained to Jim, "Taking care of the accounts is pretty boring. Sometimes we call it donkey work—but someone has to do it. And you're right! Tori and Steve should devote their efforts to catching the hacker. They're really very good at what they do."

"Hey, Pete—don't start playing Mr. Modest," Steve laughed. "Come on, buddy! You're every bit as good as we are, and you know it."

"Yeah," Tori agreed. "We'll take turns with the drudge work, Pete."

"Okay," Jim agreed. "Now that you guys have worked it out, you'd better get started. There are a couple of other things I have to check out. Maybe we'll get lucky today. Wouldn't it be great if we could put Harry out of business once and for all?"

Chapter 11

Jim headed for the library. When he told the librarian what he was looking for, she led him right to it. For the next 20 minutes, Jim was busy reading.

Next, Jim headed across the campus to Professor Anderson's office. It was in a very modern-looking building. Jim discovered that the professor shared a secretary with two other teachers.

At first, the secretary tried to protect her boss. She wasn't sure if Jim had the right to search the professor's office. "What exactly are you looking for?" she asked suspiciously.

"I'm not really sure," Jim said. "But Professor Anderson is the head of the Computer Department, isn't he? I thought I might find something about students in his files. Something that would help us figure out who the hacker is."

The secretary seemed surprised. "You think it might be one of the professor's students?"

Jim nodded. "I've studied the way the hacker writes programs. That's why I need to go through the records. It's the only way I can match up the hacker's style with a student's style."

The secretary reluctantly unlocked the door to the professor's office. "I don't think you should take anything away," she said in a huffy voice.

"I don't plan to," Jim said. "If I find what I'm looking for, I'll let you know. By the way, I understand the professor is pretty popular," he added.

The secretary smiled broadly. "Yes, he's *very* popular. Everyone likes Professor Anderson. He's a fine man and he's clever, too. Really knows his stuff."

"I hear he published an award-winning article not long ago," Jim said.

She nodded. "We're all so proud of Professor Anderson. He makes Mayfair College look good. That's what's really important to President Delaney, you know. He wants all the instructors to publish important papers in their fields of study. Then we look good, and the college attracts more money and more students."

"Publish or perish," Jim said. "I've heard of that. If teachers don't publish on a regular basis, they lose their jobs."

"Yes, I'm afraid it's a dog-eat-dog world," the secretary said with a sigh as she returned to her desk.

Jim studied Professor Anderson's office. The room wasn't much bigger than the cubicles in the Computer Security Department. A file cabinet took up one corner, and a desk and chair filled another. There were stacks of papers and books everywhere.

"How does Anderson find anything?" Jim wondered.

He began going through the file cabinet. Fortunately, Professor Anderson had kept records that went back for years. From information in these files, Jim could tell exactly when Mayfair College had first started offering computer classes. That was when Professor Anderson had been hired.

But Jim was even more interested in the students' records. He grinned when he found Steve's. His grades were great. The kid was really bright! And Tori was another outstanding student.

Jim was glad the records were in alphabetical order. That made it easier. But at the same time, he really had a lot of material to dig through.

Then, at the back of one of the drawers, Jim came across a box of hard floppies. They weren't labeled. "That's funny," Jim muttered. "Why keep blank disks hidden here?" Unless, of course, the disks weren't blank. Jim turned on the professor's computer and inserted the first floppy disk he grabbed.

Not long after that, he found what he was looking for. He was stunned to learn that his suspicions were right.

"I see it, but I don't believe it," he said softly. "Or rather, I don't *want* to believe what's right before my eyes."

But the proof was there. Now Jim knew who the hacker was.

Chapter 12

Jim found an empty manila envelope. He put the disk inside, sealing the flap with tape. Then he wrote his name on the tape. No one would be able to open the envelope without destroying the seal. He gave the envelope to the secretary for safekeeping. "I don't *care* who asks for this," Jim told her. "You may only give this envelope to me!"

Next, Jim headed right back to the hospital. He needed Ms. Clay's help. But when he told her what he wanted to do, she was reluctant to help. "Do you realize the *danger*?" she gasped.

Jim nodded. "But I think my plan is foolproof," he said. "At least I hope so!"

She finally agreed. Within the hour, Ms. Clay made an official announcement.

Professor Anderson would be moved from the college hospital to another hospital in the morning. Because of his condition, he could not have visitors.

Jim made sure that people saw him leave campus late that afternoon. He parked off campus and entered the hospital through a service door in the alley. Ms. Clay was there to meet him. She took him up the back stairs to the professor's room. They made sure that no one saw Jim enter.

"What now?" she whispered.

"Now, I wait," Jim muttered. "Let's see if someone springs the trap." He settled down in a dark corner.

Through a crack in the blinds, he could see the sky. Afternoon gave way to evening. Then Jim watched the skies darken and stars appear. He was getting hungrier by the minute. "Maybe I was wrong," he thought. "Maybe—"

Jim froze when the door opened. A shadowy figure slowly entered the room.

The figure crept to the professor's bed and leaned over. Jim saw the person pick up a pillow and start to bring it down over the professor's face.

"Hey!" Jim roared as he flipped on the lights. When the figure turned, Jim found himself staring at Pete!

At that moment, security guards poured into the room and subdued Pete.

"Meet Harry the Hacker," Jim said sourly as Pete was handcuffed. He saw the angry look on Pete's face. "I know what you did and why you did it, Pete," Jim said. "I just wish you hadn't tried to solve your problem this way."

By the next morning, the story of Pete's capture had spread like wildfire across campus. When Tori and Steve appeared in Computer Security, they were in no mood for work.

"Is it true? *Pete* was the hacker?" For the first time, Tori's mouth didn't curl into a sneer. She looked shaken.

"Yeah, tell us everything," Steve said.

"How could all of this have happened?"

"It all started last year," Jim said. "Pete wrote a brilliant paper for his computer class. Then, the next thing he knew, Professor Anderson published it himself—under his own name."

Publish or perish! President Delaney was hounding the instructor to publish something that would make the college look good. Anderson was desperate—so he stole his student's work. When Pete discovered what Anderson had done, he had threatened to go to the authorities.

Anderson warned Pete that it was Pete's word against his. If Pete made any trouble, Anderson said, he would tell the authorities that Pete had stolen the material for the article from *him*! After thinking it over, Pete decided that people would certainly take Anderson's word over his. But he was furious.

It was then that he came up with a way to strike back. Pete was an expert hacker. He had a field day breaking into the campus computers and making mischief. He knew the faculty and staff would be upset. But he also knew that most of the students would get a kick out of it. Pete saw himself as a kind of Robin Hood of the computer world.

Then Professor Anderson became ill and went into the hospital. Now Pete saw a way to do more than just make mischief. People would think he'd created the virus just to annoy the staff—but then got carried away and changed the dose of medication.

"If he *did* get caught," Jim said, "that would be his defense. Everybody was supposed to think that he changed the dosage by accident," Jim said.

"You mean that it wasn't? He *really* wanted to kill the professor?" Tori asked in amazement. Her eyes widened.

Jim nodded. "Things had gotten out of hand for Pete," Jim said. "If Anderson got well, he would have suspected Pete. The professor knew how upset Pete was.

He could easily have figured out who messed with his dosage." Jim shook his head sadly. "Pete was outraged at what Anderson had done to him. I guess it kind of drove him crazy."

"Oh, poor Pete!" Tori exclaimed.

"Yeah? Well, poor Pete was charged with attempted murder this morning," Jim snapped. "That's the real world of cybercrime, Tori."

She looked at Jim in shock.

"How did you figure it out?" Steve asked.

"It all started with something Pete said the first day I arrived," Jim said. "Remember the student reporter? Pete was trying to tell him about security and privacy. He used the example of a student stealing a research paper from another student."

Steve nodded.

"Yesterday I decided to take a look at Anderson's award-winning article. Then I went through the professor's files, looking for something to lead me to the hacker," Jim said. "That's when I found a copy of Pete's research paper on disk. It wasn't hard to see what Anderson had done. But that wasn't enough to link Pete to the attempt on Anderson's life. I still needed to catch him in the act."

Tori shuddered. "I can't believe we've been working with Pete day after day and never knew," she said.

"Professor Anderson won't be getting off the hook either," Jim said. "He stole someone else's work! That's a crime, too. He may not get any prison time, but his reputation will be ruined. And Delaney will certainly fire him!"

"Will Pete go to prison?" Tori asked.

Jim nodded. "Probably. And every day he's behind bars he'll regret what he did. How do I know? Because hacking was once *my* claim to fame!"

Steve and Tori's mouths dropped open. They stared at him in disbelief.

"You wanted to know about my

background," Jim said. "Until recently, I was in a federal prison—serving time for a cybercrime. So I know firsthand what Pete's going to experience."

"What did you do?" Tori asked.

Jim gazed at her with an impertinent grin. "What *didn't* I do!" he said. "By the time I was 15, I was hacking into all kinds of computers. I told myself it wasn't wrong because I was only doing it for fun. I was a hacker, not a cracker. I didn't destroy any files. I was like a spy who sneaks into someone's home and reads the mail."

He saw that Tori and Steve were uncomfortably shifting in their chairs. They didn't have to say anything. Jim knew what that meant. He was pretty sure they'd tried hacking a time or two.

"Then I got really bold," Jim went on. "I hacked into some government computers. But after a while, that got boring. So I went all the way and hacked into a bank's computers."

Tori gasped and stared at Jim in horror. Steve said, "You *didn't!*"

Jim straightened up. The grin disappeared. "Oh, yes I did! One thing led to another. I wanted to see what would happen if I moved some money from one account to another. Well, I soon found out! It wasn't long before FBI agents broke down my door."

Jim stood and began to pace. "You know what they called me at my trial? A *thief!* A common thief! That's when it finally sank in. I was no better than a shoplifter. No better than someone who robs a corner grocery store. Yet, there I was, thinking I was so hot! But I was nothing but a criminal!"

Tori gulped. "How long were you in prison?" she asked.

"Almost four years," Jim said. "Right now, I'm on probation. Delaney only hired me because he could pay me next to nothing. I can't get a better job because of my prison record." He paused, glancing from Tori to Steve and back again. "So now do you get it?"

They nodded solemnly.

"When I look at you two," Jim said, "I see myself a few years ago—so sure I was smarter than everybody else. I just hope you guys won't make the same mistakes that Pete and I made."

At that moment the phone rang. Tori jumped up and ran to answer it. "Cybercops Incorporated," she said, flashing a big grin at Jim.

COMPREHENSION QUESTIONS

RECALL

1. At Mayfair College, what were computer users told to change every few months?
2. Who hired Jim Salvatori to improve computer security at the college?
3. Did Jim have a good reason for refusing to talk about his background?

IDENTIFYING CHARACTERS

1. Which character was nicknamed "Bulldog"?
2. Which character liked to call Jim "Cybercop"?
3. Which character stole Pete's research paper?

DRAWING CONCLUSIONS

1. Why was Jim better qualified than everybody else to head the Computer Security Department?
2. How did most of the college students feel about tightening computer security?

NOTING DETAILS

1. What “missile” was hurled at Jim when he first arrived on campus?
2. What was unusual about Tori O’Neal’s appearance?
3. According to Jim, what did “Harry the Hacker” fail to leave behind?
4. What had Professor Anderson done that made Mayfair College “look good”?